First published 2010 by Parragon Books, Ltd.
Copyright © 2018 Cottage Door Press, LLC
5005 Newport Drive, Rolling Meadows, Illinois 60008
All Rights Reserved

10 9 8 7 6 5 4 3 2 1

ISBN 978-1-68052-546-5

Parragon Books is an imprint of Cottage Door Press, LLC.
Parragon Books® and the Parragon® logo are
registered trademarks of Cottage Door Press, LLC.

thank you
for being my friend

Peter Bently   Gill McLean

PaRragon.

It was a dark night. In the bedroom,
nothing stirred.

Nothing except a heap of bright wrapping
paper on the end of the bed.

The paper rustled.

It crackled.

It shook.

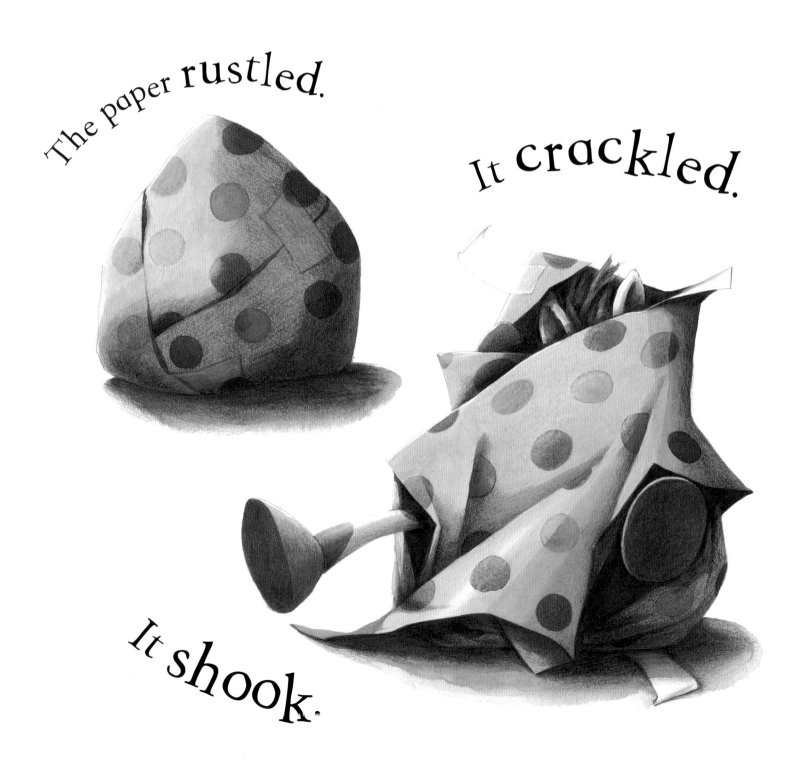

And then out jumped a toy horse.

"Hello!" said the horse. "I'm Cleo."

But there was no answer.

Cleo trotted across the bed. "Where is everybody?" she wondered, "I don't like the dark and…

Oof!"

Cleo tumbled

onto the floor.

There were strange shapes in the dark.
"I'm scared," shivered Cleo.

"I can see monsters!"

There was a thin monster...
a cuddly monster...
a tall monster...
And a monster with no head!

Cleo saw a faint gleam.
A light!
Trying not to wake any
of the monsters, she
tiptoed carefully
toward the door.

She tumbled

out onto the landing.

"Oh," said Cleo,
"it's only the moon." Suddenly
a cloud slid over the moon and
everything went dark.

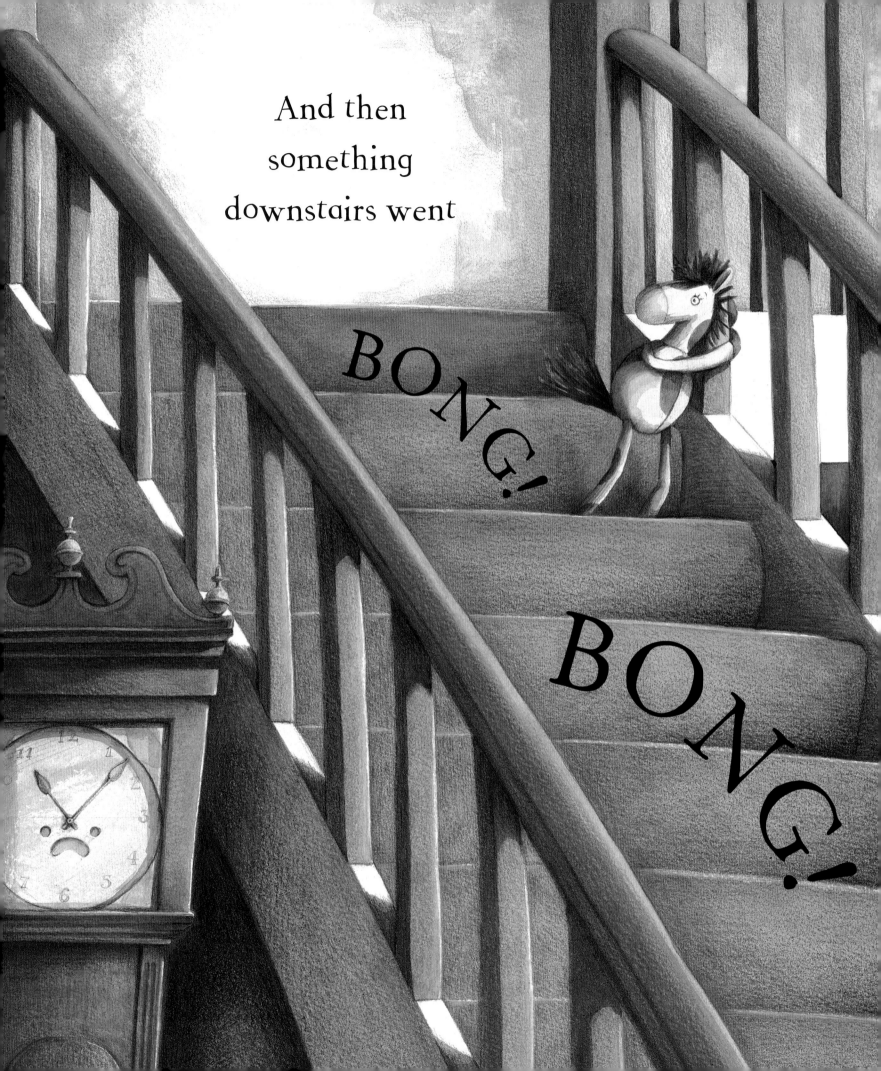

And then something downstairs went

BONG!

BONG!

Cleo nearly jumped out of her skin.
"Another monster!" she whinnied.

BONG!

BONG!

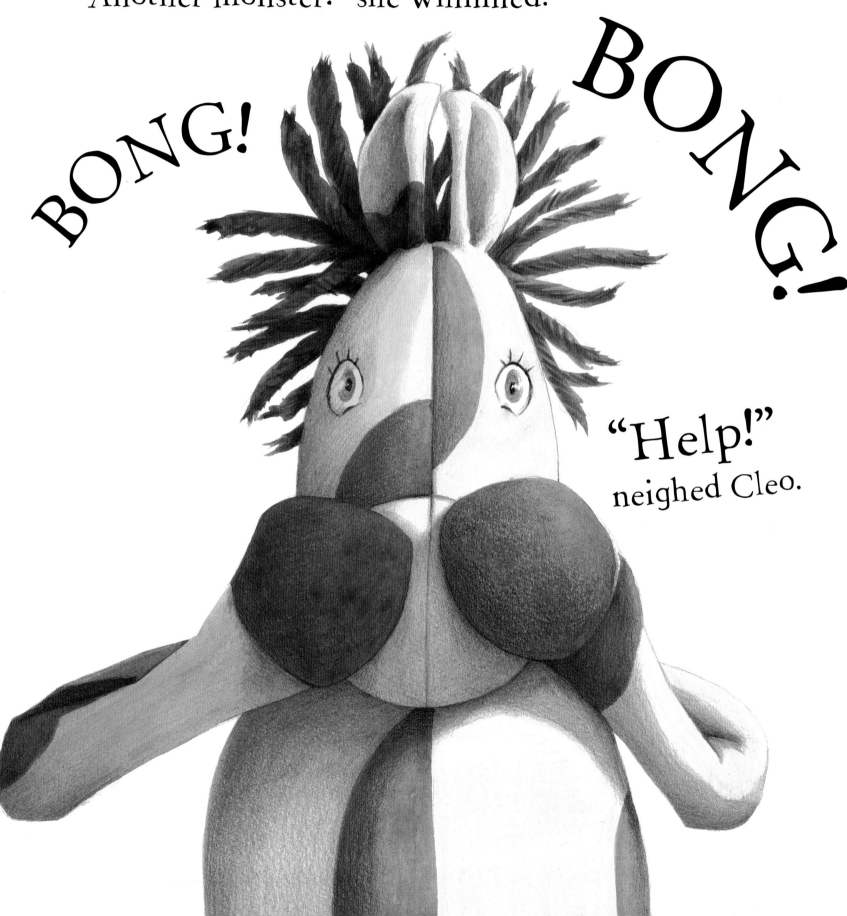

"Help!"
neighed Cleo.

Cleo spun on her hooves
and galloped back the way
she had come.

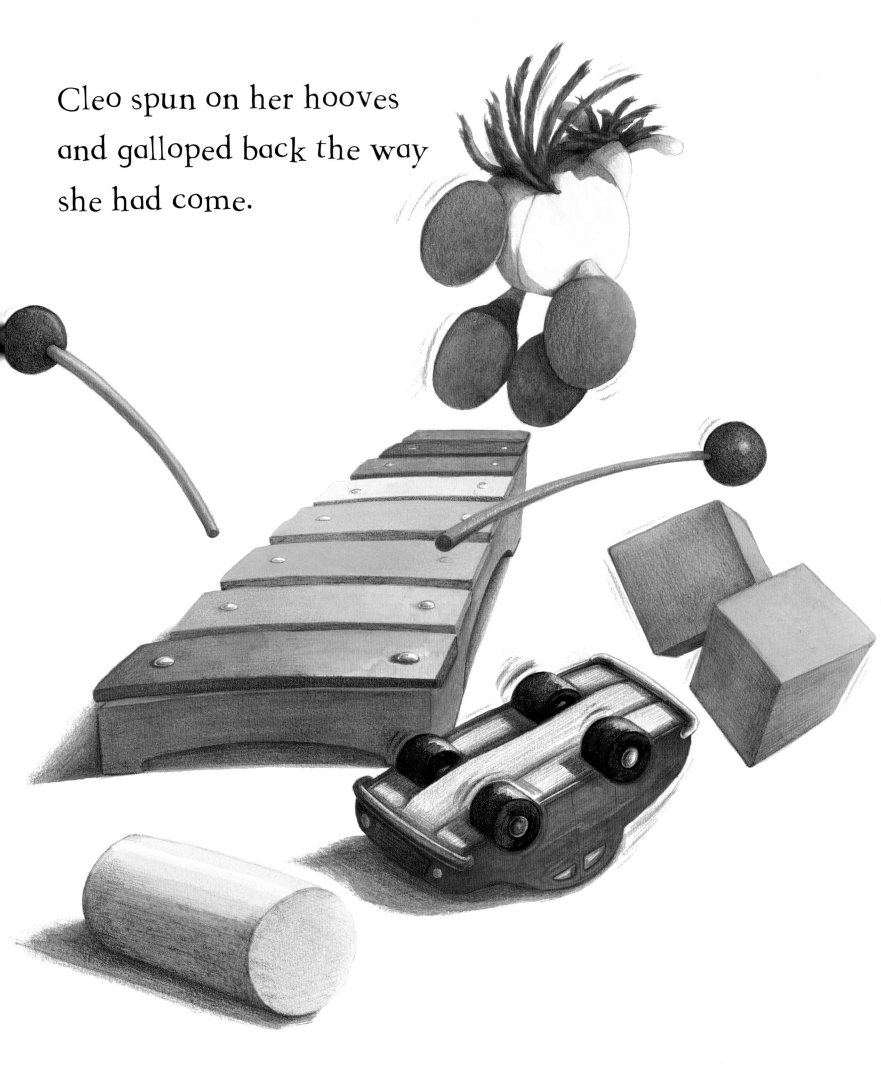

Cleo trotted into the bedroom and
tripped over something on the floor.

"Ugh," groaned the Thing drowsily. "Who... who are you?"

"I'm C-Cleo," muttered Cleo. "P-please don't eat me up!"

Then the moon came out again and Cleo saw that the Thing was a fluffy yellow duck. "I'm Daphne," smiled the duck. "And why would I want to eat you?"

Cleo told Daphne all about the monsters.

"The monsters won't hurt you," said Daphne.

"Promise?" asked Cleo with a big yawn.

"Promise," said Daphne kindly. "Why don't you snuggle in with me?"

"You won't go, will you?" said Cleo.

"No. You're safe now. Good night," said Daphne.

Good night!

The next morning, Cleo peeped out
from under Daphne's wing.
She blinked in the bright sunlight.
"Morning sleepyhead,"
quacked Daphne.
"Come and meet all the monsters!"

Cleo shot back under Daphne's wing.
"Don't worry," laughed Daphne.
"They won't eat you,
I promised, remember."

The thin monster was…

a lamp!

The cuddly monster was…

a pile of cushions!

The tall monster was… a wardrobe!

And the headless monster was…

a dressing gown!

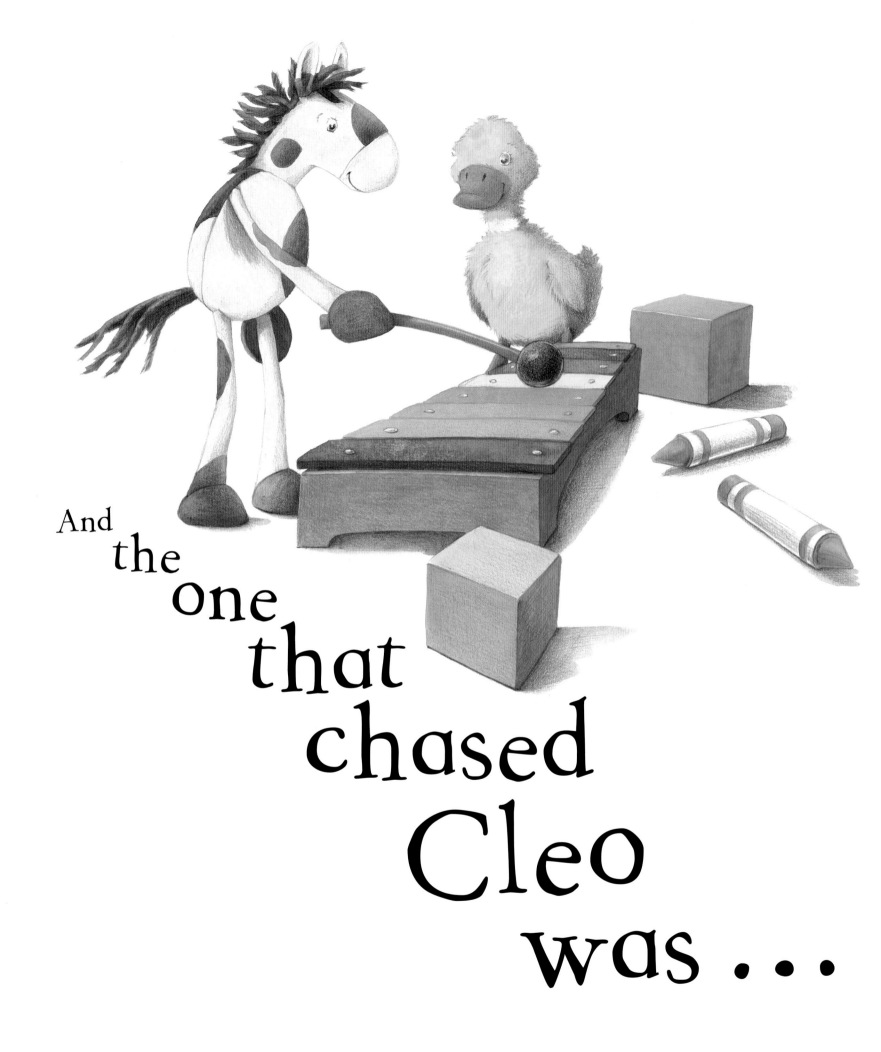

And the one that chased Cleo was . . .

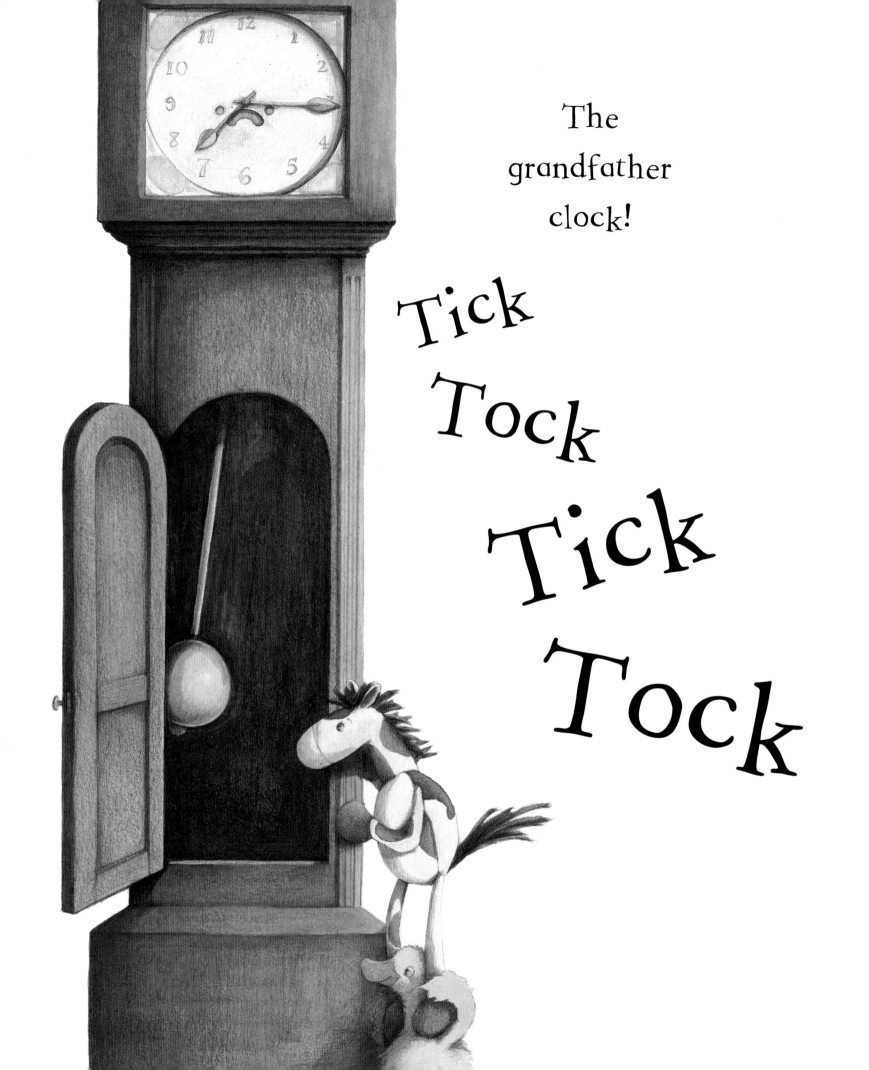

The grandfather clock!

Tick Tock Tick Tock

"I've been really silly," smiled Cleo.
"No, you haven't," said Daphne.
"Lots of things look more scary in the dark."

"I don't think I'll be scared anymore,"
said Cleo. "Now that you're my friend."

The end